WHO IS IN MY TUB?

by Mary Packard

Illustrated by David Olsen

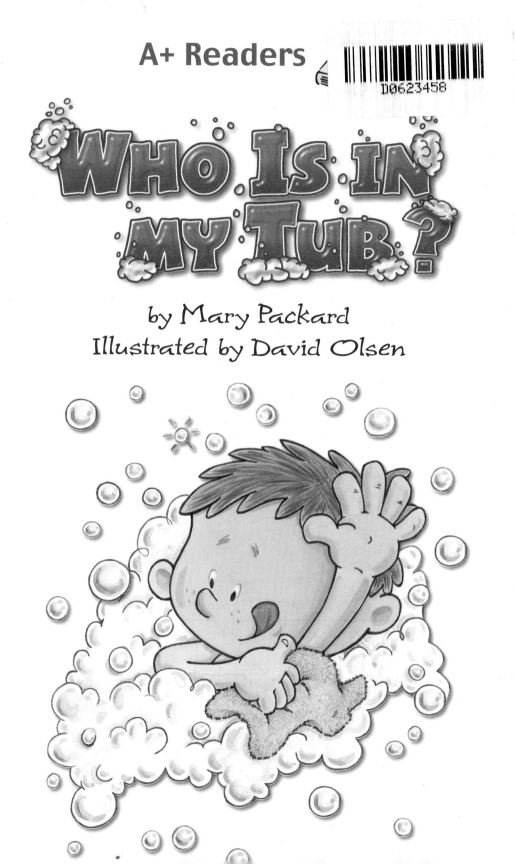

Rub-a-dub-dub!
See the bubbles in my tub?

Hey! Who is that I see?
Someone's in the tub with me!

6

Does he have big eyes for staring?
Does he have sharp claws for scaring?

Does he live inside a shell?
It's so dark, it's hard to tell.

Could I ride him on the sea,
slow and steady as can be?

Would he take me for a spin
while I hold his flat tail fin?

Does he glow with shiny scales?
Or does he have a spiky sail?

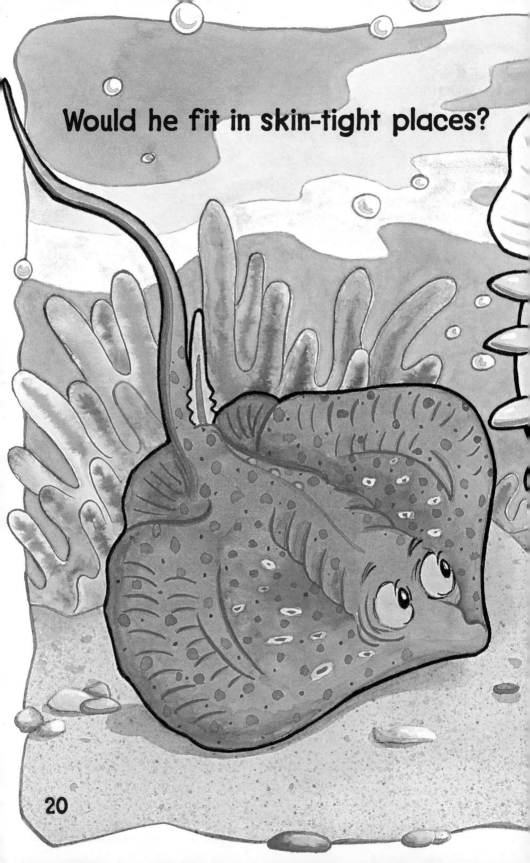

Would he fit in skin-tight places?

20

Or does he need
wide open spaces?

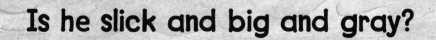

Is he slick and big and gray?

22

Do you think he likes to spray?

Does he float upon his back
while he eats a seafood snack?

25

Do you think he needs a shave?

Would he like to ride a wave?

Or would he like to play
in my bubble bath all day...

so we could rub-a-dub-dub...
in my warm and soapy tub!